HENRY AND AMY
(Right-way-round and upside down)

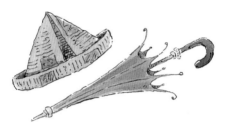

For
Brother Dave
(Sandy &
Imogen)
and
Sister Mel
(Tyrone)

Miranda and
Charlotte,
(Mandy
& Pam)

Mark
and Liz,
(Hannah)

Trish
and Tani

Scholastic Press is an imprint of the SCHOLASTIC GROUP

Sydney • Auckland • New York • Toronto • London

King, Stephen Michael.
    Henry and Amy (right-way-round and upside down).

    ISBN 1 86388 997 3.

    I. Title.

A823.3

Text and illustrations copyright © Stephen Michael King, 1998.

First published in 1998 by Scholastic Australia Pty Limited
ACN 000 614 577, PO Box 579, Gosford 2250. Also in Sydney,
Brisbane, Melbourne, Adelaide and Perth.
www.scholastic.com.au

Stephen Michael King used watercolours and black ink for the
illustrations in this book.

Typeset in Modified Fontesque Bold.

Printed in Hong Kong.

9 8 7 6 5 4 3 2 1   89 / 9

HENRY AND AMY

(Right-way-round and upside down)

Story and pictures by

Stephen Michael King

SCHOLASTIC PRESS

Every time Henry tried
to draw a straight line . . .

it

turned

out

wiggly.

When everyone around him looked up . . .

Henry
looked
down.

If he thought it was going
to be a beautiful sunny day . . .

it would rain.

Splish

Splash

Sploosh

Early one morning when Henry
was out walking backwards,
trying very hard to walk forwards,

he bumped into Amy.

Amy could do everything right.

She *never* tied her shoe laces together

or buttered the wrong side of her toast.

She always remembered her umbrella

and could write her very own name.

Henry thought everything Amy did was amazing.

So Amy showed him his **right** from his **left**,

his front from his back,

and that the sky was up
and the ground was down.

One day they decided
to build a treehouse.

Amy worked on a plan so that
it would sit in the tree just right.

Henry added lots of squiggly wiggly
bits that made them both giggle.

Deep down, Amy wished everything she did wasn't so perfect.

So Henry found
her a coat and a hat
that didn't match.

Then he taught Amy
back-to-front

and
topsy turvy.

They rolled down a hill sideways . . .

and together they
learnt how to fly.

Henry and Amy are the
very, very best of friends . . .

right-way-round

and upside down.